Arya's
Flying
Dreams

by Nagma Dawn Datt
illustrated by Valerie Bouthyette

Ark House Kids
PO Box 1722, Port Orchard, WA 98366 USA
PO Box 1321, Mona Vale NSW 1660 Australia
PO Box 318 334, West Harbour, Auckland 0661 New Zealand
arkhousekids.com

This is a work of fiction. Names, characters, places and incidents are either the product of the author's imagination or are used fictitiously.

Cataloguing in Publication Data:
Title: Arya's Flying Dreams
ISBN: 9780648670308 (hdbk)
Subjects: Children; Fiction;

Design and layout by www.initiateagency.com
Illustrated by Valerie Bouthyette

For all little people with big

dreams.

Especially my kids,
nieces and nephews.

Your wings already exist.

All you have to do is fly!

Arya **dreams** about flying.

Like a bird...like a plane...

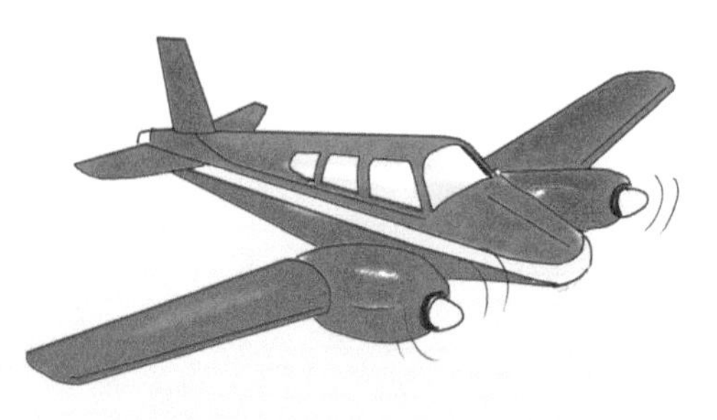

or like Superman!

Early one morning he decides to make his dreams come true.

He sticks some bird feathers onto his arms and climbs onto a low, sturdy branch of the tree in his backyard.

Then he spreads his arms out wide like the wings of a bird and leaps into the air.

Instead of swooping
high like a bird,
Arya falls like an acorn
from the tree
onto the trampoline below!
He tries again and
again but he just cannot
fly like a bird.

Mum suggests eating breakfast
might help him to think
of more ideas.

While he eats breakfast,
a bright idea POPS
into his mind.
He also feels much
bigger.

After breakfast Arya puts his idea into action.

He sticks two long pieces of cardboard onto both his arms and balances on the branch of the tree.

Then he opens his arms out wide like the wings of a plane and leaps into the air.

Instead of zooming
through the air like a plane,
he falls like an apple
from a tree...
onto the trampoline!
He tries again
and again but
he just cannot
fly like a plane.

Mum suggests eating lunch might help
boost his brain power.

As he eats lunch, a

new idea

flashes into his mind.

He also feels much **stronger.**

After lunch, Arya prepares to try and fly again.

He paints a big 'S' on his favourite blanket, ties it around his neck like a cape

and climbs

onto the branch of the tree

Then he straightens his arms out in front of him like Superman and leaps into the air.

Instead of soaring through
the air like Superman,
he falls like a coconut
falling from the tree...
onto the trampoline below!
He tries again and
again but he just
cannot fly like
Superman.

Arya and Mum agree that he **tried** very hard to fly all day. Mum suggests eating dinner might help give him **energy** to try one last time for the day.

While he eats dinner, his mind is
busy inventing.
He also feels very
energised.

After dinner, Arya carries his mum's scarf onto the trampoline and holds the ends of the scarf in each hand.

Then he lifts the scarf above his head, opens his arms out wide and bounces

high into the air.

This time he glides down onto the trampoline, like he is wearing a parachute.

Bouncing high into the air and gliding down onto the trampoline

almost feels like flying!

He has so much fun doing this, again and again.

At bed time, Mum is glad to hear about how much fun he had today. She wishes him a good night's sleep so that he is fresh in the morning to invent more ways to fly.

She knew his dreams would take flight!

That night, Arya dreams about flying when he grows even bigger, stronger and inventive.

Perhaps he will *fly* a hot air balloon, a helicopter or a rocket ship!

“ ”

Never let it be said that to dream is a waste of one’s time, for dreams are our realities in waiting. In dreams, we plant the seeds of our future.

- Author Unknown

Dawn is passionate about reading and writing meaningful stories, whilst raising her three kids, together with her husband in Melbourne. Dawn is a member of Writer’s Victoria and writes regularly on her blog, www.CreativeMama.com.au. She aspires to empower parents with insights to have fun connecting creatively with their kids.